Kathleen &
Victoria,
Hope to see you
one day soon!
Your Friend,
Donald

The Peabody ®
ORLANDO

Preferred
HOTELS & RESORTS

Donald Tompkins
Duckmaster

9801 International Drive, Orlando, Florida 32819
407.352.4000   fax 407.345.4500
email: duckmaster@peabodyorlando.com
www.peabodyorlando.com

Think Pink

Think Pink

By Olga Cossi

Illustrated by
Lea Anne Clarke

PELICAN PUBLISHING COMPANY
Gretna 1994

*To my granddaughters, Michelle and Autumn,
of whom I have great expectations*

*The word "Pelican" and the depiction of a pelican are
trademarks of Pelican Publishing Company, Inc., and are
registered in the U.S. Patent and Trademark Office.*

Library of Congress Cataloging-in-Publication Data

Cossi, Olga.
    Think pink / Olga Cossi ; illustrated by Lea Anne Clarke.
        p.   cm.
    Summary: Debbie Duck is a popular attraction at the Peabody
Orlando Hotel, until her fascination with anything pink threatens
her stay there.
    ISBN 0-88289-995-3
    1. Ducks—Juvenile fiction. [1. Ducks—Fiction] I. Clarke,
Lea Anne, ill. II. Title.
PZ10.3.C8197Th 1994
[E]—dc20
                                                                    93-5556
                                                                      CIP
                                                                       AC

The Peabody Orlando and Peabody Duck names are owned by Belz
Enterprises, Inc., and are used by permission.

Manufactured in China

Published by Pelican Publishing Company, Inc.
1101 Monroe Street, Gretna, Louisiana 70053

THINK PINK

Debbie Duck lived in the Royal Duck Palace on the recreation roof of The Peabody Orlando Hotel in the city of Orlando, Florida. At eleven o'clock each morning, she led a troupe of four other wild ducks to their special elevator that took them down two stories to the main lobby of the hotel.

When the elevator door opened, a John Philip Sousa marching song began to play, and Debbie and her troupe did their famous Royal Duck March along a red carpet to the marble fountain in the middle of the lobby.

"Way to go!" shouted the crowd of children waiting beside the red carpet. They loved the famous "March of The Peabody Ducks" and came every morning to watch. They laughed and cheered as the row of wild ducks waddled by and splashed into the fountain.

At five o'clock that afternoon, the band music started playing again. Down went the red carpet and Debbie and her troupe marched back to their elevator and up two stories to the Royal Duck Palace where they spent the night.

Debbie was very proud of being a Peabody Orlando Duck. She loved the excitement of the Duck March and the children who came to watch. She always did exactly what the kindly Duck Master taught her to do, and never left the fountain nor wandered off the red carpet.

But early one morning, something happened that almost ended her career as a Peabody Orlando Duck. That morning when Debbie opened her eyes, the sun was just coming up. It turned the sky a soft, rosy pink. Soon the very air was pink. Even the clouds turned the delicious color of cotton candy.

Debbie was delighted. Just like that, she began to "think pink." Her heart beat faster, her feathers stood on end, and her eyeballs quivered. When it was time for the Duck Master to open the door to the Royal Duck Palace so she could lead the Duck March, she was still thinking pink.

That afternoon, while Debbie was swimming around in the marble fountain, a little girl walked by eating a pink, strawberry ice-cream cone. Before she could stop herself, Debbie began to think pink. Her heart beat faster, her feathers stood on end, and her eyeballs quivered.

She forgot about her training for the Duck March. She forgot that she was never to wander off the red carpet nor leave the beautiful marble fountain. Off she went, leaving a trail of wet duckprints as she followed the little girl across the lobby.

"Quack! Quack!" called Debbie, waddling as fast as her short legs could carry her.

"What a friendly duck!" exclaimed the little girl. "Would you like some ice cream?" She held the cone so Debbie could reach it.

Debbie was about to take a big bite when the Duck Master saw her. Now, being the Duck Master meant that he was responsible for the safety of all the ducks in the Duck March, including Debbie. He knew that it was not safe for her to be wandering around the hotel. What if she accidentally got locked in the luggage room? Or what if she went out the front door and got in the way of the cars?

"I'm glad I found you, Debbie!" the Duck Master exclaimed as he escorted her back to the fountain. "Peabody Ducks are so popular I thought maybe one of the hotel guests had taken you home with him. I hope you haven't forgotten how special you are to me, and to the troupe."

Debbie had indeed forgotten. She felt awful. She hung her head and waddled back into the water with the other ducks.

She was just beginning to feel good about herself again when a bellman went by carrying a huge bouquet of pink orchids. Debbie tried her best to look the other way, but before she could stop herself, her heart beat faster, her feathers stood on end, her eyeballs quivered, and she began to think pink.

"Quack! Quack!" she called, hurrying after the bellman.

"Would you like one of these pink orchids?" asked the bellman when he saw Debbie following him.

Just as Debbie was about to pick out an orchid for herself, the Duck Master was counting the ducks in the marble fountain. One of them was missing! Then he saw Debbie with the bellman and the bouquet of pink orchids at the far end of the lobby. He couldn't believe she was out of the fountain again. He hurried over and gently scooped her up.

"Are you sure you are OK?" he asked, stroking Debbie's well-groomed feathers.

The Duck Master had been training Peabody Orlando Ducks for years. He couldn't remember any of them acting like this before. He lowered Debbie into the fountain and watched her swim away.

Debbie was just beginning to feel like herself again when a cloud of pink lace floated past the marble fountain. Three bridesmaids dressed in long pink gowns were walking by. Debbie's heart beat faster, her feathers stood on end, and her eyeballs quivered as she began to think pink again.

"Quack! Quack!" she called, hurrying after the bridesmaids.

"Look! There's a duck following us!" giggled one of the bridesmaids. She leaned over and petted Debbie's smooth head. "Would you like to be part of our wedding party?"

Debbie was so pleased she quacked louder than ever.

The bridesmaids were as pleased as Debbie. "You can be our flower girl," they said. They placed a pink bow on the top of her head and gave her a basket of pink roses to carry. Then they took her with them to the chapel where the wedding was to be held.

When the wedding march began, Debbie waddled up the aisle, leading the three bridesmaids.

Everyone thought Debbie was the cutest flower girl they had ever seen. She plucked pink roses out of her basket with her beak and scattered them along the aisle.

Meanwhile, back in the lobby, the Duck Master counted the ducks in the fountain and saw one of them was missing again.

"It must be Debbie!" he told himself. "Now where can she be?"

He looked by the reception desk. He looked in the elevators. He looked outside the front entrance. He began to worry. Debbie was nowhere to be seen.

He was wondering where to look next when he heard the sound of the wedding march coming from the chapel. Could Debbie be in there? It seemed like a wild idea, but, after all, Debbie *was* doing wild things lately.

As quietly as he could, he opened the chapel door and peeked inside. There was Debbie standing beside the bride and groom with her basket of pink roses!

The Duck Master couldn't help smiling. Despite his concern for her safety, he thought she was a sight to see. He waited until the wedding ceremony was over before he scooped her up and carried her back to the water fountain.

"This is really too much," sighed the Duck Master, as he took the pink ribbon off Debbie's head. "Maybe you are just tired. I'm going to have to take you back to the duck farm for a rest and let one of the other trained hens lead the Duck March."

When the hotel guests heard what he said, they knew they had to help. Without Debbie leading the troupe, the Duck March would not be the same. What could they do?

At last one of the guests had an idea. Everyone was sure it would work. They promised to meet on the recreation roof of the hotel before the Duck March started the following day.

Just before eleven o'clock the next morning, the hotel guests were waiting when the door to the Royal Duck Palace opened. They had a surprise for Debbie—a pair of bright pink sunglasses. The Duck Master nodded with approval as they tied the sunglasses in place on Debbie's head with a pink ribbon.

Debbie couldn't believe her eyes. Everything she saw was pink. The sky was pink, the clouds were pink, and even the guests were the delicious color of cotton candy. Debbie was delighted. Now she could think pink all she wanted to without leaving her beautiful marble fountain in the middle of the lobby.

And to this day, when children go to the city of Orlando, Florida, to see the famous Duck March at The Peabody Orlando Hotel, the happy little duck wearing pink sunglasses and leading the troupe is Debbie.

If Debbie and her pink sunglasses are not there, then she is probably on vacation in Memphis, Tennessee, where there is another Peabody Hotel with its own famous Duck March twice a day.

But that's another story!